75x75

=

Flash Fraction

Helena Mallett

Helena Mallett has a 100 word story *Death and Life* included in the anthology *Pod and more small fiction* published by Leaf Books in 2011.
She is a Londoner currently living in the hills of West Wales.

All rights reserved. No part of this publication may be reproduced or transmitted in any form or by any means without written permission of the author.

All the characters in this book are fictitious and any likeness to any real person, living or dead, is coincidental.

ISBN 978-0-9574026-0-7

Copyright © Helena Mallett 2012

Published by Marsh Cottage Publishing 2012

www.helenamallett.com

Contents

1. The Knock
2. Blush
3. The Vanishing
4. Are You Sure?
5. Ignore
6. Sunday Roast
7. Red Earth
8. The Conversation of Men
9. All I Want For Christmas
10. Ghost Story
11. The Ex's New Girlfriend
12. A Moment Of Beauty
13. Two Blonde Women
14. Amsterdam
15. Shut Her Up
16. At The Funeral
17. Wee Cough
18. Back To The Land
19. Looking Good
20. Birthday

21. Still Got It
22. Boy's Own Boy
23. Chapel And Cowshed
24. A & E
25. How About India
26. Dead Skin
27. The Cut
28. Hot
29. Valentine
30. Absent Son
31. Football
32. Forbidden Love
33. Autumnal Autopsy
34. The Old Hand
35. Forbidden Revenge
36. Desert Love
37. Goodbye
38. Gang Girl
39. Hands
40. Head First
41. Too Late
42. I Know You Want To

43. A Date With Death
44. This Time
45. In The Woods
46. Old Bag
47. It's Time Now
48. Tube
49. Lady Fortune
50. That's The Kick
51. Last Ferry
52. The Hand
53. Last Piss
54. Iron
55. Mother And Son
56. No Return
57. North And South
58. Nothing To Stop Us Now
59. Not Now
60. Swell
61. Taut Trousers
62. Pale Shuffle
63. Peeing In The Dark
64. Picture

65. Private Messages
66. Fear
67. Rain And Chips
68. Soap Opera
69. Simple Things Really
70. Spellbound
71. Tsunami
72. The Cap
73. Tipi
74. Tommy's
75. The End

The Knock

She sees there's snow falling as she draws curtains over white ghost-like impressions on the darkening windows. Christmas Eve, and there's always a certain poignancy. It's a family time, a time to think of those not with us. Or those we've never known.

She remembers his tiny newborn body. The condemning cries as she places him in another's waiting arms, as if already angry, blaming.

There's a sudden knock at the old cottage door.

'Mum?'

Blush

Margaret's 70th birthday celebrations take an unexpected turn when she's introduced to Jim. Tall, tanned and handsome, his teasing blue eyes awaken Margaret's latent mischievous sense of fun and soon their joined laughter rings out across the hot summer's night. A few days later Margaret enters a high street salon with trepidation.

'I'd like a full beauty treatment please. Wash and blow dry, full facial, manicure and,' lowering her eyes and blushing slightly, 'a Brazilian.'

The Vanishing

Joey hates visiting Grandma, especially for Christmas. A dark old house in the middle of nowhere with her weird paintings of extraterrestrials smothering every wall; spooks him out a bit if he's honest.

Now there's a bloody power cut and the old girl's telling yet another of her alien stories. He's had enough; she's clearly off her rocker.

He steps outside to clear his head in the cold night air and is never seen again.

Are You Sure?

'Are you sure you want to do this?'

'Yes, but let's take it real slow. One step at a time.'

'We don't have to do it now you know. We can wait ...'

'No. I'm ready. It's just that it's been a while and at our age ...well I'm worried you won't want me afterwards.'

'I will. I promise.'

And still the consummate professional, the safebreaker kneels to slowly and skilfully pick the Sultan's lock.

Ignore

I log on to Facebook.

Her friend request surprises me.

We were young and crazy together, pushed every social and sexual boundary.

It's a simple message.

'Hi, I see you married John then! We must meet up.'

Her cyber presence shakes me. It's so long ago and I've grown middle-aged. A little heavy perhaps, but content.

I don't want John to see her again.

I click 'Ignore'.

And besides, she always was far too thin.

Sunday Roast

I'm serving up the Sunday Roast when he asks if I'm sleeping with Joel.

I turn out the Yorkshire puds. Perfect.

'No, of course not. No. What on earth makes you ask that?'

A roasting tray slips and tilts slightly between guilty hands. I find it hard to meet his eyes.

'I've seen how you are together. I'm not blind.'

'Look I'm not, but even if I was, Dad, it's really none of your business.'

Red Earth

Janie pats down the last of the Devonshire red soil and looks on with smug satisfaction. She's won. Having weeded and wrenched the last of the sharp stubborn brambles, in their place she's sculpted a perfectly hexagonal flower bed. The paved patio path will now weave villagers directly to the perfumed area on her open garden day.

She particularly likes that his sadistic rotting corpse will be so approved of and admired in this way.

The Conversation of Men

A freshly-lit fire draws the two old friends close, inviting a familiar intimacy as they share their customary Sunday evening pint. From a deep and comfortable silence that perhaps only men can know, Mark says, 'So you've asked her to marry you then?'

'Aye. I have.' Paul sighs, lifting a hand to raise his glass.

And such is the conversation of men as a fire crackles, bar girls laugh and Ozzy plays on the jukebox.

All I Want For Christmas

High up on the hill it's quiet but for the sheep and occasional plane flying overhead. Birds swarm in a blue winter sky. Underfoot, the last of crisp, white snow, while across the ridge, the age-old sound of a rhythmic tap, tap, tap as a farmer fixes his fence.

Moments later this idyllic timeless scene turns suddenly surreal as a farmer's mobile phone rings out across the hills: 'All I Want For Christmas Is You.'

Ghost Story

The snow's six feet deep and drifting when there's an unexpected knock at the cabin door. I've not heard them arrive in the muffled silence but understand why when I see the elderly couple hovering on my porch.

'Please, don't be scared. We used to live here.'

'Come on in. I'm glad of company.'

We sit around the fire where instead of telling my usual ghost stories, I enjoy an evening of … ghosts' stories.

The Ex's New Girlfriend

I hear your car drive up the track. Still the same sleek purring Alfa after all these years. I didn't expect you to bring her here. Not today.

She's blonde, spray-tanned and over-dressed. Hangs on to every word as she clings to your arm, tottering precariously on ridiculous high heels in the battering West Wales wind. I don't anticipate her warm hug or friendly smile. I really don't want to like her. But I do.

A Moment Of Beauty

It's a moment of beauty as doors open wide to erupt with a huge, colourful, vibrant surge of child energy. The multi-coloured mass of Christian crosses, Jewish caps, dreadlocks, hijabs, bindis and Rasta hats dance before my eyes.

No matter in this moment that they say different prayers, eat different foods, may later divide. For now, as black hand holds white, it's a precious moment of innocence and hope in this inner city London school.

Two Blonde Women

Across the darkened room there's a cosy candlelit dinner for two. He watches the two blonde women holding hands and gazing into each other's eyes. She's not looked at him like that for a long time.

'Cindy?'

'Jim! What are you doing here?'

'Well I could ask you the same thing. What's going on?'

'Er…'

'Tell me please … who is this?'

She swallows and takes a deep breath.

'Jim, this is our daughter Candy.'

Amsterdam

He walks slowly through the tree-lined canalside streets, an old man now with greying hair and pacemaker ticking, timing his life. He enters the café, takes a pipe in his hands. Watches all life pass by, content. There are times he promises others, that it's over, and he will no longer go back.

But this love affair runs deep, this mother of all love affairs, still pulling him back to the dope-filled cafés of Amsterdam.

Shut Her Up

'Put the rubbish out, love, will you?'

'Yeah, in a minute.'

'And don't forget to phone Steph.'

'I'll do it after the Football.'

'And we need to talk.'

'Oh give me a fucking break, it's Sunday.'

'Don't be like that. I hardly see you all week, there's stuff to sort out.'

'Like what?'

'Like stuff. Family stuff.'

He really has to shut her up before the match.

'Hello? Is that Cake Hole? Do you deliver?'

At The Funeral

A black skullcapped rabbi sings in the old language, his virtuous voice lilting through high vaulted rooms. An outsider here, I stand with doll-like women, their geisha girl faces and stick-thin figures balanced perilously on stilted heels.

I watch my dear friend grieve and stumble over ancient Hebrew words, and as he throws the London clay to bury his new loss, we feel a generational autumnal chill … for we are now next in line.

Wee Cough

The couple lie in bed, hot under an African sun.

'We need to go back to Scotland. Dad's obviously ill again. Mum says he has the wee cough.'

'But the bairns, and work…'

'Sorry love, I thought he was in remission. We have to go.'

***

They stand suntanned and cold on the frozen Edinburgh street. His father answers the door.

'Dad!' You look really well?'

'Aye Son, I am. I have the week off.'

Back To The Land

Later tonight lambs will be born where, a few hours before, we stand watching the black bellies hang heavy in the late afternoon light. Before this we are drinking tea from ancient china cups, as we discuss the girl's portrait hanging on your wall. I search for words, momentarily discombobulated as I discern you wringing the chicken's neck with such ease, spilling its bright red blood back to the land …and then I remember.

Looking Good

I'm looking good and know it; three decades older than most here, slim, toned and with sun-bleached hair against my dark tanned skin, many of the young lads are turning their heads. I adjust my new bikini and walk down to the sea. The blond lifeguard watches me. I like that.

'You alright?' he winks as I walk back feeling sexy, water-swept, 'We have to keep an eye on you older ones in this heat.'

Birthday

It's my eldest son's birthday today. He dismisses my greetings. It's just another day. He will work late.

So long ago, yet I remember with such clarity the waves of that primeval, ancestral pain of birth that links all women together. Easy for me now to recapture the view over London from high up on the third floor and that final miracle of joy as my son's first cry sounds out over a Hampstead dawn.

Still Got It

She looks in the mirror. She's lied slightly about her age. He probably has too. They all do.

Is pink too brash? Is black too sober? She wonders what he's like. He sounded nice online. She'll straighten her hair and go for the blue. Oh, and the killer high heels and new red lipstick. That'll do the trick.

He simply throws on old, faded chinos, with his favourite shirt and thinks, 'Yeah, still got it.'

Boy's Own Boy

I'm thirteen and invincible. The original Boy's Own boy. It's a vinyl black night but this wild old wood's my personal playground. So what if it's spooked. Bring it on.

'What the Fuck?'

The hooded white shape comes at me fast. Pincer claws grab my neck but I throw an air punch straight through and run.

Next morning there's the blown tarpaulin and fallen tree … but I can still feel the fear even now.

Chapel And Cowshed

We gather quietly, maybe a hundred or so, to say goodbye in the old chapel. It is as if I too am on the threshold of another world, as I watch this unknown close-knit community support and share in their loss.

The solemn service is surreal as disrespecting cows moo from a nearby shed, and then cloaked in the black shrouds of grief, we cry openly as we bury you deep in this ancient ground.

A & E

The six of us are only together for an hour. It's a hot sultry night in the busy A & E and we're all feeling the heat. Moments before we'd been crossing roads, cooking barbecues and making love; but now there's fresh blood on the floor and a smell of vomit nearby.

'Polly Johnson please?'

'Yes.' I stand with difficulty.

I'm astonished when several hours later I hold a beautiful baby girl in my arms.

How About India

'How about India?' she asks lazily.

'Why India?' I feel familiar jolts of jealousy jackknife in my stomach.

'Why not?'

She knows she's challenging me, forcing me on to dangerous ground.

'You know why not. Because he's there.'

'It's over Raj. I'm with you now. I'd like us to visit the family.'

I love her too much to lose her again … and so I say nothing of the deleted emails I found in Trash.

Dead Skin

Sometimes I find fine flaky fragments of your dead skin scattered across the dashboard of the car. I hold them gently between frail, failing fingers and think back to the solid bulky shape they used to form. And as I remember your big bear hug holding me tight, so vital and warm, it seems impossible that you can now be reduced to these tiny transitory grey ashes that will one day all be blown away.

The Cut

She holds them in her hands, unaware of their power and the enormity and spectrum of emotions they evoke in me. She lifts them slowly. Our eyes meet. In the mirror, she sees my fear and desperation. She starts to cut. I shut my eyes. I can barely look.

And then suddenly it's over and I'm happily booking another appointment as I hand her a ridiculously sized tip of relief and leave the new salon.

Hot

It is hot. An afternoon hangs suspended and timeless in a drone of tractors and bees. The three of us sit in a row with our backs to the sun. We are decades apart. All of us ill.

I wonder momentarily, who will be the first of us to go, and imagine the almost apathetic ease of drifting, without fight, to become one with the humming afternoon and soporific sun.

I wake and make tea.

Valentine

Two pairs of retired, middle-aged hands open Husband and Wife Valentine cards. She accepts the customary red rose. He's booked their usual table.

Alerted by a distinct rumble outside, the grey-haired man rises … looks with wistful envy at the young, bleached-blonde lad riding a Harley-Davidson. Black Sportster, low-slung handlebars, shiny silver chrome shimmering in the sunlight. Classic.

'Now there's a fine Harley,' he nods.

'Happy Valentine's Day, darling,' she says, handing him the keys.

Absent Son

'Go on treat yourself, darling, all real leather. A wallet for him, a purse for her, only a tenner,' grins the tall, good-looking young lad with perfectly perched cap and confident, cheeky smile. She knows him well. He used to sell flowers on Baker Street all through that long cold winter. Now he's bagged himself a prime pitch up on the main drag.

He looks okay, a little thin. She wishes he'd come back home.

Football

I'm understanding when he talks of training, managers and selection. After all, it's only every four years. And it is England. I'm even supportive when he fills the supermarket trolley with beers, pizza and cigarettes, for of course there'll be tension with all those free kicks, corners, saves and near misses.

The impossible happens. England are out. He's inconsolable. I comfort and reassure, crack open cans to commiserate.

And now it's all about … Brazil.

Forbidden Love

Two men sit on hot golden sands under Allah's relentless sun. They watch the burqa-clad women, Grim Reapers of His desert, as they twist and turn in perpetual timid motion to make the final preparations for their weddings.

Forbidden fingers touch lightly under white dishdasha robes as they try to imagine the silhouetted shapes become partners, lovers and mothers; these hooded and hidden strangers who will soon share their beds and destroy a forbidden love.

Autumnal Autopsy

He moves closer to pick over the broken bones of our dying, decaying love, as he conducts his own personal, autumnal autopsy. The sea of red, gold and brown leaves are in sharp contrast to the shades of grey and black between us that he now depicts in such painstaking detail as he leafs through our story book, page by page, extinguishing, anecdoting and blaming, until I feel nothing but the sun on my skin.

The Old Hand

The weekly support group gathers as seats are sought with nervous hands and hesitant smiles. They offer names in the age-old, round-robin way.

A grey-haired man introduces himself, somewhat aloof and arrogant, for he's an old hand at this game. But his heart stops dead, when against the backdrop of London taxi brakes and clearing fog outside, a beautiful girl looks him straight in the eyes and says, 'My name's Sarah and I'm your daughter.'

Forbidden Revenge

It's happening every night now; I have to stop him. I imagine his contorted, twitching face as he becomes the wide-eyed vulnerable victim, while I look on triumphant, relentless in my forbidden revenge.

'Are you scared?' my brother asks as we mix the poison.

'No.'

But we both jump as the front door slams behind our animal-loving, hippy parents who would be horrified if they knew their children were plotting … to kill a mouse.

Desert Love

Ours is illicit, unstoppable, dangerous love. We risk our lives.

Under a desert sun, hidden by bronze boulders' shadows, we ride the crest of our personal tsunami. I sense danger but am too high on the swell to stop, and it's only afterwards as I watch the shimmering shards of light find small places through dry cracked stones that I'm sure they're there, and that we are now the hunted.

High above, the vultures circle.

Goodbye

We meet in the old Welsh graveyard. A sea fog hangs heavy and silent, obscuring the looming, lifeless grey tombs. Your sister weeps as she tells ancestral stories of those who gave you life and who now lie silent in this death-filled ground.

As I hold and comfort her, I do not say that I was last to hear your screams or that it was I who cold-bloodedly and dispassionately ignored your plea for life.

Gang Girl

'Sure you wanna do this?'

'Yeah, I'm sure.'

'You scared?'

'No.'

'That's my baby.'

'You'll still love me after though? Promise?'

'I'll ask Rosie if you don't want to.'

'No. I do.'

'There'll be eight or so … you know most of them.'

'Yeah I know.'

'And then you'll belong babe … be one of us and we'll take care of everything.'

'Yeah.'

She thinks of the status, the bling … and walks slowly in.

Hands

Cawing crows screech over old cathedral walls as sun shines down on green blanket lawns. Locals and tourists share the early summer's day. Inside, a Botticellian cellist plays sweet, sonorous sonatas to the small clustered congregation. Pushing through heavy oak doors I find the warmth of an unexpected crowd, and see his picturesque, patchwork paintings.

She, however, paints of you with bloodied death on your hands, although they are almost clean when you hold mine.

Head First

It's dark and warm here as I drift … lazy and foetal-like against smooth, nurturing membrane. Nearby, rhythmic thumping sounds out like a jungle drum, quickening as smooth skin edges closer. My head feels trapped; I'm suddenly fighting for survival as I push and propel downwards to black. Instinctively I ride the swelling wave and we are one when it breaks. Yes, I'm going now. Head first.

I'm a heavy baby, eight pounds nine apparently.

Too Late

He forces a last unwanted mouthful down in the busy hospital canteen. On the first floor directly above where he now sits, a beautiful wife reaches for his ever-present, absent hand to hold. But he doesn't know this as she takes her final gasping life-breaths. Yet he feels a sudden cold chill in the hot oppressive air as he enters the lit-up lift to press the button that will take him to her early death.

I Know You Want To

'I know you want to.'

'No. I don't.'

'I won't tell.'

Our eyes lock. My stomach tightens under a professional pose. I shift my body slightly in the well-worn therapist's chair.

'We've talked this through. It's impossible. It will never happen.'

'Oh it will …'

'Our sessions and all contact must end today.'

'But it won't. We both know that. It's inevitable now.'

I know he's right. I know we will. I have everything to lose.

A Date With Death

I don't know him well – perhaps an occasional chat over the photocopier or query about holidays and sick pay. But today we are talking of death.

'Do you believe in any kind of afterlife?' I ask, ever curious of the great unknown.

'No. And to be honest I don't really care. I just wish I knew the exact date of my death so I could organise my pension precisely.'

'Huh?'

'What?' Is that really anal?'

This Time

I'm nervous as my supportive husband holds my hand, soothing and concerned. From high above me a voice says, 'Just relax, you'll feel a little prick' and I let the strong sedative take me away.

I drift and dream of children. Twin girls. I watch them climb sweet smelling fruit-laden trees in a summer garden, open gift-filled stockings, excited and impatient on Christmas Day.

'All done,' the voice says. 'There's two strong embryos this time.'

In The Woods

I hear his heavy-booted, thudding thumps and run into the dark dense woods. Twigs crushed under my fleeing feet echo out like gruesome gunshot in the crisp frosty night. Killer-happy hands and rank panting breath are close by as I cling to bare branches that trick me into tight strangling hands.

Years later as I hold the yellowed press cutting between old shaking hands, I'm in awe of the bravery of that ten-year-old, small-town girl.

Old Bag

'What d'you mean you're leaving me? How can you? And today?'

'Linz …'

'You're gonna leave ME for HER? That fat, ugly, depressing old bag. She's so HORRIBLE …'

'Lindy…'

'What the HELL d'you see in her? You've always said you don't like her and that Peter should leave the bloody witch. And all the fucking times I was there through all their marriage shit …'

She stops to breathe …

'It's not Petra,' he says.

'What?'

'It's Peter.'

It's Time Now

His day, as always is long. Back at the flat there's the usual heaps of embraced then discarded clothes strewn across a shared bedroom floor. In the bathroom, half-open bottles of shampoo and herbal oils spill over the small glass shelf and her long black hairs spike around the bath like delicate broken spiders' webs.

The phone rings.

'It's time now, Jim. We must clear out her stuff. It's been three months since she's gone.'

Tube

The tube is delayed but at last the sea of twitching, tutting commuters moves with a collective sigh of relief as the red Circle Line appears, shunting and snake-like, from the dark mouth of a tunnel. Squashed against blackened windows and wrapped around multi-fingermarked poles we press against bodies of strangers in a way that would be dangerous, perhaps sexual elsewhere, but here the boundaries are different as we play our consensual game of Twister.

Lady Fortune

Lady Fortune, absent for so long, is back. She smiles benevolently, offering her profuse apologies and promising prolific pecuniary gifts. He worships and believes in her as he grips his dead-cert ticket, sees the food-filled fridge, big TV, new car.

But moments later outside the betting shop on the Kilburn High Road, the wife drops to her knees as she hears the broken man's cries.

'They moved the fucking line. They moved the fucking line.'

That's The Kick

It's hot in here tonight. We wrap around fluorescent pulsing poles and make calculated eye contact with the group of balding businessmen, hoping we'll be their final deals of the day to close.

My pulse races when I see him come in. I know he likes to watch me. I'm dangerous and forbidden. But that's the kick.

Tomorrow we'll talk of children over our shared garden fence. The four of us may even have dinner.

Last Ferry

We watch as the afternoon ferry shunts and shifts across the glass sea to Ireland. I stand as always upon our special rock, while you sit frail now, a blanket over your knees. We gaze together as so many times before, until our eyes, the ferry and hazy horizon merge together to become one shimmering, swirling mass of blue-white.

Tomorrow I will watch this scene alone for you shall not last the night they say.

The Hand

She swears the hand had grabbed her, wrapping its clutching fingers around her neck as she ran through the empty afternoon park. She's badly shaken and crying.

'It's on me, it's still here!' she screams.

I'm horrified. I imagine evil spirits, demonic beings. I console and comfort, make her drink hot sweet tea.

Days later, I recognise her photograph in the local paper and see she's been admitted to hospital after an overdose of LSD.

Last Piss

The alleyway's dark and pumped-up in anticipation. It echoes with your filthy phlegm-filled rasping cough and heavy breathing. I watch with disgust as your familiar bulbous belly flops and flaps over the top of ancient dirt-stained trousers, lowered now to release an arc of stinking yellow toxic piss, briefly illuminated by a car's passing headlights. A sudden siren sounds from an oblivious ambulance.

Gun poised, I wait. Even I won't deny you a last piss.

Iron

If I hadn't seen it with my own eyes …

She arrives in work late. Tells me she has a bad hangover. I laugh. I'm head down, working.

'And I was sick on the tube.'

'Oh?'

'And I've gone and bloody ironed myself!'

I look up.

'What!'

'I was late … so I just ironed through my clothes.'

And there under bright office lights she lifts her skirt to reveal the unmistakable imprint of an iron.

Mother And Son

Late afternoon sun slants over the Sunday table where mother and son eat. They dissect skillfully, lifting the almost raw red meat from bloodied bones, as in shared olfactory expectancy, they raise poised forks into salivating open mouths. During intermittent pauses they discuss the cut, whether from neck or leg or perhaps the age of the lamb.

Conjoined in this discussing and dissecting, they are oblivious as I gag slightly on my cashew nut roast.

No Return

I'm surprised when Tom, his twin, joins us. The three of us had been together earlier on the beach and as a hot summer sun glinted down on matching macho muscles, I had wondered briefly if perhaps I'd chosen the wrong one.

It's later, as James and I are kissing and heading towards that point of no return when I feel Tom's unexpected touch and shiver.

'So, have you had a threesome before?' he asks.

North And South

I flirt briefly with the south of the county as we delight in cream teas under cherry blossoms and marvel at the green growth of sunnier climes. I imagine arriving for dinner by boat and sailing back under night stars to a regal riverside home.

But where else would my heart miss a beat at the beauty of rising hills, recognise friends' footprints in freshly fallen snow or have neighbours that feed foxes by moonlight?

Nothing To Stop Us Now

'Look Lucy, I love you. I always have. And there's nothing to stop us now.'

'I don't know … I …'

'Why not? What's changed?'

'Please Chris, not now …'

She grips and slips nervous fingers on a steering wheel, replaying the images of yesterday afternoon for the thousandth time; the sweet scent of hyacinths, the fading afternoon light as it fell across a first tentative testing touch.

She'll phone Sue later. They'll tell him together.

Not Now

'Not now,' she says, 'Not here.'

He persists, 'Why? Cherie, why?'

Winter rain lashes at steamed-up windows of the South Hampstead café, where others not in the final throws of a mortal marriage, consume cappuccinos and chocolate croissants.

Brushing hair from jaded resigned eyes, she looks to the man approaching the table to say, 'Well if you must know, because I'm having lunch with my lover.'

'Phil, this is John', she says wearily, 'John, Phil.'

Swell

Sun beats down on dark dots of black driftwood as they wait, rocking gently on the moving mass of blue-green, jelly-like water. As the ocean's belly rumbles and rises to a roaring crescendo, they spring to life, standing tall and poised on treasured boards. They ride the prime crests, in the prime of their lives, exhilarated and at one with the sun and crashing white foam, before all is quiet, and the cycle starts again.

Taut Trousers

He knows he shouldn't touch but she's so damned pretty. A mixture of innocence and coquettish coyness. Just the way he likes them. He trembles on the bridge of tantalising temptation; pushes clenched hands into taut trouser pockets.

And then he is holding her. Caressing the soft and forbidden. Inhaling the sweet succulent smell of new youth to satiate his brazen desiring body.

Sod the allergic reaction. This kitten's worth it a thousand times over.

Pale Shuffle

'What about this one?'

'Which one now?'

'Look, I'm really trying and it's not helping you being like this.'

'Like what?'

'You know, still being funny about…'

'I'm not.'

'You are.'

'Well if you hadn't…'

'Yeah, well I'm sorry. And I told you it was only once for God's sake.'

'Yeah, but in the bed our kids were born? How could you do that?'

The good-looking salesman meets beseeching blue eyes, pales and shuffles away.

Peeing In The Dark

When our German driver sells his bus in Kabul we cross the Khyber Pass in a rusty old Ford Transit van. We leave the vibrant multi-coloured trucks of Afghanistan for the clamour and callings to prayer of Islamic Pakistan, and then on into India, my own personal holy grail.

It's a life-changing adventure over perilous, precarious mountain passes, yet my overriding memory now, is of peeing in a dark Indian night, with wild buffalo nearby.

Picture

Sometimes I lay here and imagine your conversations.

'I love you.' I might hear you say, or, 'I'll leave soon, after Christmas.'

'I'll wait,' she whispers lovingly.

At other times it's the age-old lover's tiff. 'If you loved me you'd leave.'

'Please, don't start.'

I replay the scenes obsessively, over and over, until I make myself sick with jealousy and exhaustion.

Yet I can never quite picture you both here together in our marital bed.

Private Messages

It's all pretty innocent at first. You know how it is. You share the occasional comment about football, politics, perhaps some old music ... post stuff on each other's walls.

Thirty years on and her profile pic shows the same piercing blue eyes and thick dark hair.

My wife doesn't suspect a thing and when I get the first private message I see no real harm in replying.

But of course it doesn't stop there.

Fear

My heart's beating way too fast; two terrified hands are clenched, left with right, tight and white. I forget to breathe and draw fresh red blood from my son's steady hold. His youthful face appears calm and brave, but others here are wide-eyed and watchful as we collectively share this unnatural, nature-defying moment.

The deep rumbling escalates then deafens as we hear a ferocious fusion in the roaring engines of an easyJet take-off to Barcelona.

Rain And Chips

I lie in the golden sand dunes and listen to grasses swaying. Sun beats down from a holiday sky. Wealthy accents drift on the breeze as they talk of boats, second homes and ding-dong meals.

I grow restless and wander over to the more exposed expanse of windswept beach where with immense nostalgia I watch families build their annual sand-castles and hear warm, friendly Northern accents talk of caravans, rain and chips. This is better.

Soap Opera

He waves a remote control impatiently in my direction. I'm blocking the view of his favourite soap opera. Evening air hangs heavy with the pregnant silence of a stagnant marriage. We sigh in unison. He turns away to watch others' lives.

'I'll be going then.'

There's no answer as I pack rudimentary remnants of our shared decades, close the family door behind me and walk.

For we shall live and star in different soaps now.

Simple Things Really

Simple things really. Rise slowly, push up from arms on the chair, feet steady onto the floor. Pashmina, slippers, stick, glasses, cup, book. Turn the TV off at plug. Lounge light off but leave the hall light on. Glass of water from the kitchen and check the cooker's switched off. Put phone, stick, water and book by bed. Turn back the sheets. Lamp light on, the main light off. Yes, simple things really. Ninety tomorrow.

Spellbound

I'm already under her spell when she says, 'Quick, we must hurry' and our sunbathed, sea-salted hands join for the first time. We run through the old Gothic quarter, down dark narrow alleyways under a sliver of silky silver moon.

'Look, there!' she says, pointing to a billowing soundless shape floating across the old Spanish square.

I freeze. I'm terrified.

Later, after we're lovers, she laughs, telling me she's props manager at a local theatre.

Tsunami

Mother Earth shudders, spewing wave after wave of unthinkable magnitude. The unstoppable indiscriminate tsunami swipes and splays broken bodies and man-made detritus at random. I watch as white suits, face masks and Geiger counters are shown against a backdrop of burning nuclear reactors and desperation-driven hurtling helicopters circle and spray water, attempting to avert further, unprecedented disaster.

And all of this, all of this here … in the land where cherry trees wait to bloom.

The Cap

She's always hated the cap.

'It looks ridiculous on you. I don't know why you're so attached to it. I'm giving it to charity.'

Of course this was before he was ill, lost and wandering in the ravages of his cruel, crucifying illness.

I watch my mother now as she smoothes down my father's once-thick black hair and places the cap gently upon his head.

He has no awareness of this final act of love.

Tipi

They sit cross-legged and expectant in the circle. Hands are cupped and tipped open to receive the energies and wisdoms of other worthier worlds. But all I hear is the West Wales wind and rain battering relentlessly against our holy silence on billowing canvas walls of a tipi. I sneak a peek through narrowed eyes as the special 'chosen ones' speak in strange tongues to offer channelled messages from beyond.

Not to me they don't.

Tommy's

'Mum. I'm pregnant.'

'But you can't be. You're only sixteen. Are you sure?'

'Yes, I'm sure. I'm sorry. I know I've let you down.'

'How far gone are you?'

'Three months.'

'And does the father know?'

'Yes.'

'And?'

'We want to keep it.'

'And how will you manage that?'

'He works. He'll support us both. We've talked it through.'

But this was nothing compared to what I had to tell her next.

'It's our Tommy's.'

75 x 75 = Flash Fraction

The End

'So what's this book you're writing?'

'75 x 75.'

'Huh?'

'It's 75 stories, each 75 words long.'

'What? You tell a whole story in just 75 words?'

'Well, I try. I guess some are more like snapshot moments of life rather than stories … but yes, I hope I manage to take the reader somewhere.'

'How do you start? Straight in with a story?'

'Yep.'

'And how do you finish?'

'With a full stop'

.

www.helenamallett.com

Printed in Great Britain
by Amazon.co.uk, Ltd.,
Marston Gate.